BILLY MONSTERS

Monsters
at the Beach

ZANNA DAVIDSON

Illustrated by MELANIE WILLIAMSON

Reading consultant: Alison Kelly

Meet Billy...

Billy was just
an ordinary boy
living an ordinary
life, until
ONE NIGHT
he found
five
MINI
MONSTERS
in his sock drawer.

Gloop Peep Fang-Face Captain Snott Trumpet

Then he saved their lives, and they swore never to leave him.

We give you the Secret-Hairy-Snot-Tooth Oath of Devotion.

When he moved, Billy found ANOTHER monster.

Hello. My name's Sparkle-Boogey.

One thing was certain – Billy's life would never be the same AGAIN...

Contents

Chapter 1
Sun and Sand

It was Saturday and the Mini Monsters were very excited. They were going to the beach.

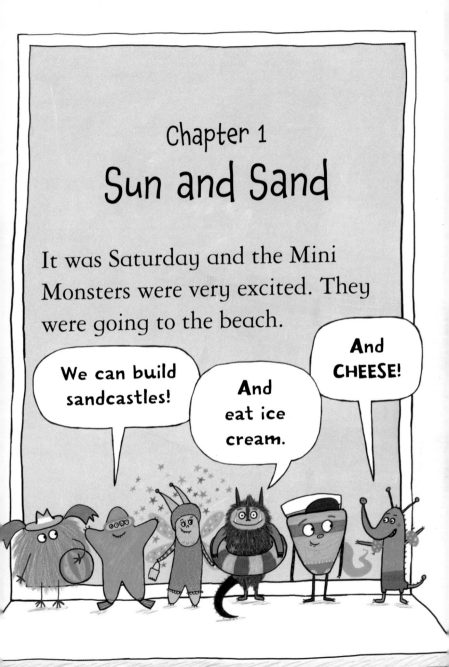

We can build sandcastles!

And eat ice cream.

And CHEESE!

Billy's family was also very excited about their trip.

Billy's dad was looking forward to doing some birdwatching.

Billy's mom wanted to go sailing.

Billy's sister, Ruby, couldn't wait to swim in the ocean.

In fact, everyone
was excited...

EXCEPT Billy.

Billy **really** didn't
want to go.

"Why don't you like the beach?" asked Gloop.

"I don't like the way the sand gets **everywhere**," said Billy.

"It gets in my socks."

"It gets in my SANDwiches."

"And," Billy went on, "the sea is full of

POISONOUS CREATURES!"

"To make things even worse, Mom always takes us out in a little boat.

It goes up···

and down····

up···

and down···

···and it makes me feel sick."

"I'm not sure about the beach, either," whispered Peep. He was thinking of all the SCARY THINGS that might happen to him...

like being chased by sharks...

...and getting buried in sand.

"We're going to have an **AMAZING** time," said Billy's sister, Ruby, coming into the room with Sparkle-Boogey. "Look what we've got..."

Ruby bought them at the dollhouse shop.

"Wow!" said
the other Mini Monsters.
"I know!" said Sparkle-Boogey.
"We're all set! Isn't this fun?"

Do you like
my swimsuit?

Do you like
my goggles?

Billy and Peep looked at each other. "I suppose the beach *might* be fun," sighed Peep.

We'll just avoid boats.

And sand.

Then Billy and Ruby heard their parents calling them from downstairs.

"Time to go."

Billy scooped up the Mini Monsters and popped them in his backpack.

Trumpet? Did you bring any cheese with you?

It smells like your cheese-powered toots in here.

I don't have any cheese.

Billy ran down the stairs and jumped in the car.

And off they went...

15

16

17

19

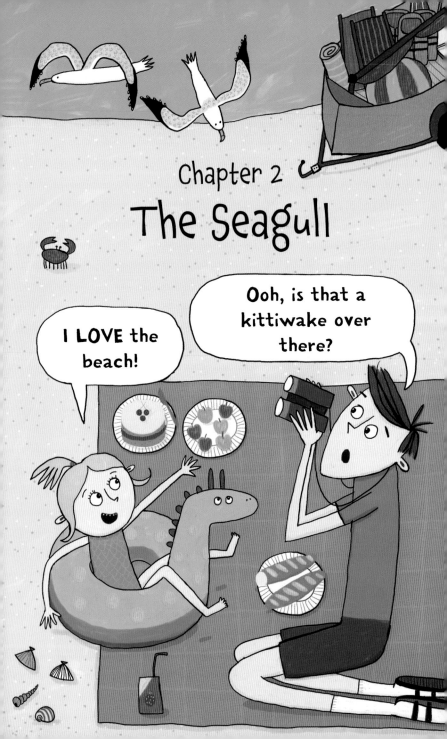

As soon as the Mini Monsters were safely hidden behind a rock, Billy and Ruby sat down for the picnic.

Let's eat!

"Isn't this wonderful," said Billy's mom. "So relaxing." Billy looked over to see Fang-Face giving him a thumbs-up sign from the side of the rock.

This is the life!

We should have picnics every day.

"Maybe the beach isn't so bad, after all," Billy thought.

He could hear the waves crashing against the shore and the seagulls cawing on the wind.

One seagull landed on the beach near them.

That's a herring gull.

It's got a very sharp beak...

The gull came closer... and closer. Then it **snatched** a cookie from the picnic and **gobbled** it down.

23

As the gull
began to hop away,
Billy's dad opened up his bird book
and Billy went over to look.

"They're not scared of humans," Billy's dad went on. "They'll even steal food from people's hands."

Herring Gull

The herring gull is a large, noisy gull with a pale gray back and wings and black and white wingtips.

Length: 21 - 26 in
Wingspan: 53 - 57 in
Habitat: coasts & cities
Diet: fish, other birds, eggs, trash

Just then, Billy heard a small cry. It came from behind the rock.

Billy suddenly had a
DREADFUL thought:
What if the gull was trying to
eat his Mini Monsters?
He ran around the rock.

There was…

Captain Snott
and
Fang-Face…

and Sparkle-Boogey…

and Peep and
Gloop…

They all started jumping up and down and pointing to a large gull in the sky.

"WHAT'S GOING ON?" cried Billy.

"WHERE'S TRUMPET?"

"He's been **stolen**!" said the Mini Monsters. "By a **BIRD**!"

29

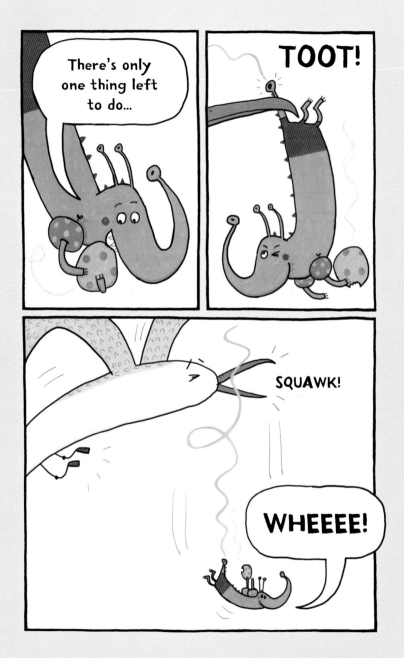

There's only one thing left to do...

TOOT!

SQUAWK!

WHEEEE!

Chapter 3
Out to Sea!

Billy gazed through his dad's binoculars. "I can see the gull! And Trumpet!" he cried.

Behind the rock, the Mini Monsters were deep in discussion.

Are we going out there too?

Yes! We're going to build a raft of our own!

38

39

40

41

Chapter 4
The Boat Trip

"I thought you didn't like going out in the boat," said Billy's mom, as they set off across the water. "It's great that you've changed your mind."

Isn't this fun?

Mmm.

"What's going on?" whispered Ruby. "I know you still hate boats. Why did you ask Mom to take us out?"

"It's **Trumpet**," Billy whispered back. "He's somewhere on the rocks. We have to get Mom to take us there. But I can't think how."

"Dad!" said Ruby. "What's that huge bird flying over there?"

"Where?"

"By those rocks. It had stripes on its wings and a yellow head."

Ooh, maybe it's a gannet! I didn't know there were gannets here.

"Quick, let's sail that way!"

said Dad, excitedly.

"Where are the other Mini Monsters?" whispered Ruby.

"They're safe on the beach," said Billy.

"Um… are you sure about that?"

Billy turned to see where Ruby was pointing. "Oh no!" he groaned.

There were the Mini Monsters, on a tiny raft, riding the **waves**.

The raft was coming straight towards them. Billy leaned down, reaching out towards the Mini Monsters.

The wave rose up and up and up and…

splashed all over **Billy**.

46

The Mini Monsters landed on the bottom of the boat.

"Where's Fang-Face?" asked Billy.

The raft was too heavy so he stayed behind.

We want to help find Trumpet.

I wish I'd stayed behind.

Billy looked **ANXIOUSLY** at his Mini Monsters. "This is a dangerous mission," he said.

47

"But I suppose we need all the help we can get. Trumpet could be anywhere on those rocks. So," Billy went on, "here's the plan…"

When we land, Mini Monsters search the shoreline!

I'll look by the cliffs.

Ruby, you search the rocks in the middle.

"Do you think Trumpet's okay?" Ruby asked Billy.

48

But before Billy could reply, Peep shook his head.

Trumpet could be hanging from a cliff!

Or trapped in a nest.

Or maybe he's been blown away on the wind.

At last, the boat reached a little bank on the far shore. Billy and Ruby jumped out onto the rocks. "We can only stay for about twenty minutes. After that, the tide will turn," said their mom.

I'm going to stay in the boat, but Dad will keep an eye on you.

BILLY GULPED. "Only twenty minutes to rescue Trumpet. And then I have to get back on that boat again…

Let's pretend we want to go tide-pooling.

Okay. I hope our plan works.

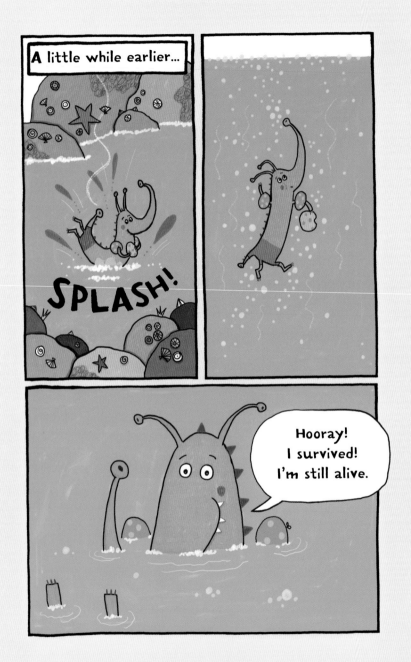

A little while earlier...

SPLASH!

Hooray!
I survived!
I'm still alive.

52

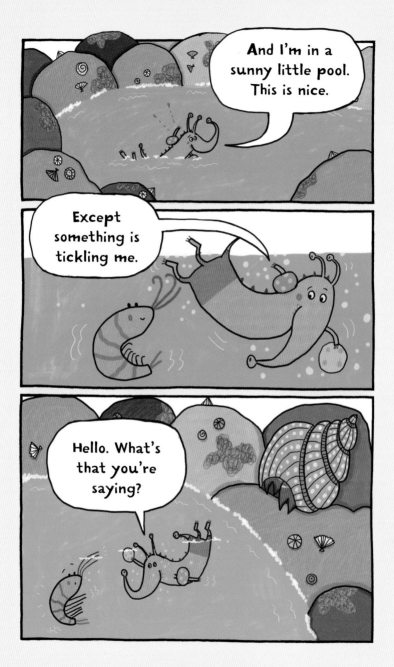

53

There's something behind me? Is that it?

It's just a shell.

Chapter 5
Sea Monsters

"Remember the plan," Billy whispered to everyone. "And Mini Monsters – make sure you stick together."

"Don't go too far!" Billy's mom called after them. "We won't," said Billy, as he secretly dropped the Mini Monsters next to a tide pool.

Billy ran towards the cliffs, his eyes darting left and right.

These rocks are huge!

"Trumpet!" he called as he searched.

How will I ever find Trumpet?

Trumpet!

But there was no answer.

Billy hunted high and low for what seemed like forever, but he couldn't find Trumpet. "Any luck?" he called over to Ruby.

"No!" Ruby called back. "I can't see him anywhere."

Maybe the Mini Monsters have found him.

But when Billy and Ruby reached the shore, there was no sign of **ANY** of the Mini Monsters.

This is a **DISASTER**.

"I'm the worst monster-keeper EVER," said Billy. "And it'll be time to go soon. The tide is starting to come in."

"You can't give up now," said Ruby. "Let's start looking in the tide pools." She set off.

"Over here!"

she cried suddenly. "I think I've found Captain Snott."

I got stuck in the seaweed.

"And there's Sparkle-Boogey," said Billy.

What happened to you?

I made friends with a starfish.

"And here's Peep," said Ruby, spotting a moving shell.

Is it safe to come out now?

"But what about Gloop?" said Billy. "I think he's still in the tide pool," said Captain Snott. "I last saw him talking to a blobby sea creature. With **TENTACLES**."

"Oh no!" said Billy. "That sounds like a sea anemone. They've got

STINGING TENTACLES."

Billy bent down to look in the tide pool again.

"I think I can see his legs," cried Billy, excitedly.

He grabbed hold of Gloop's **wiggling legs** and **pulled him** out.

Are you okay, Gloop?

"That was **strange**," said Gloop. "A funny creature was waving at me, so I went to say hello. Then it started sucking me in. Do you think it wanted to be friends?"

Maybe I should go back and say goodbye?

No, Gloop. It wanted to **EAT YOU**.

"And we still haven't found Trumpet," said Billy. "Billy! Ruby!" called their parents.

68

Come on, ducky. Follow the cheese!

Chapter 6
Together Again

I wonder where that gannet went?

Um... yes. I wonder too.

Billy arrived back at the beach feeling very sad and very seasick.

Then he heard a **quacking noise** behind him.

Billy turned around.

There was Trumpet. On a duck! As Trumpet leaped ashore, Billy gave him the best hug he could manage without squashing him.

Billy, Ruby and the Mini Monsters ran back to the rock.

There was Fang-Face, waiting for them.

Hooray!

"I'm sorry I ever brought you to the beach," said Billy. "I've put you all in terrible danger."

"And, Billy," added Captain Snott, "you went out on a boat to save Trumpet, even though you get really seasick. That was amazing."

Three cheers for Billy and the beach!

"What about you, Peep?" asked Billy.

"I still **DON'T LIKE** sand," said Peep, shaking himself out.

75

Then Billy heard his mom calling him. "I'm so glad you love the boat now, Billy," she said.

All about the MINI MONSTERS

CAPTAIN SNOTT →

LIKES EATING: boogeys.

SPECIAL SKILL:
can glow in the dark.

SCARE FACTOR: 5/10

← GLOOP

LIKES EATING: cake.

SPECIAL SKILL:
very stre-e-e-e-tchy.
Gloop can also swallow his own
eyeballs and make them reappear
on any part of his body.

SCARE FACTOR: 4/10

FANG-FACE →

LIKES EATING:
socks, school ties, paper, or
anything that comes his way.

SPECIAL SKILL:
has massive fangs.

SCARE FACTOR: 9/10

TRUMPET →

LIKES EATING: cheese.

SPECIAL SKILL:
amazingly powerful
cheese-powered toots.

SCARE FACTOR:
7/10

(taking into
account his toots)

PEEP

LIKES EATING: very small flies.

SPECIAL SKILL: can fly (but
not very far, or very well).

SCARE FACTOR:
0/10 (unless you're afraid of
small hairy things)

SPARKLE-BOOGEY →

LIKES EATING:
glitter and boogeys.

SPECIAL SKILL:
can shoot out
clouds of glitter.

SCARE FACTOR:
5/10 (if you're scared of
pink sparkly glitter)

Series editor: Becky Walker
Designed by Brenda Cole
Cover design by Hannah Cobley
Americanization editor: Carrie Armstrong

First published in 2019 by Usborne Publishing Ltd., Usborne House,
83-85 Saffron Hill, London EC1N 8RT, England. www.usborne.com
Copyright © 2019, Usborne Publishing Ltd. AE

All rights reserved. No part of this publication may be reproduced,
stored in a retrieval system or transmitted in any form or by any
means, electronic, mechanical, photocopying, recording or otherwise,
without the prior permission of the publisher. The name Usborne
and the devices ⚲ 🎈 are Trade Marks of Usborne Publishing Ltd.